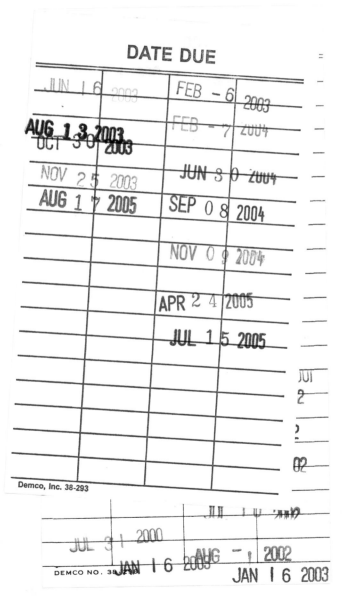

Blaze and Thunderbolt

BLAZE AND THUNDERBOLT

BY C. W. ANDERSON

ALADDIN BOOKS
MACMILLAN PUBLISHING COMPANY   New York
MAXWELL MACMILLAN CANADA   Toronto
MAXWELL MACMILLAN INTERNATIONAL   New York   Oxford   Singapore   Sydney

First Aladdin Books edition 1993
Copyright © 1955, by Macmillan Publishing Co., Inc.
Copyright renewed 1983 by Phyllis Anderson Wood

Aladdin Books   Maxwell Macmillan Canada, Inc.
Macmillan Publishing Company   1200 Eglinton Avenue East
866 Third Avenue   Suite 200
New York, NY 10022   Don Mills, Ontario M3C 3N1

Macmillan Publishing Company is part of the Maxwell Communication Group of Companies.

Printed in the United States of America
10   9   8   7   6   5   4   3

Library of Congress Cataloging-in-Publication Data
Anderson, C. W. (Clarence William), date.
Blaze and Thunderbolt / by C.W. Anderson.
p.   cm.
Summary: Billy and his loyal pony Blaze attempt to tame the wild horse Thunderbolt.
ISBN 0-689-71712-1
[1. Horses—Fiction.   2. Ponies—Fiction.]   I. Title.
PZ7.A524Blf   1993
[E]—dc20   92-27153

To Stephen Wood

Billy was a little boy who had a pony named Blaze that he loved very much. One summer when his father and mother decided to spend a vacation on a ranch in the west they bought a trailer so that Blaze could go along too. Billy enjoyed the trip across country very much. Perhaps Blaze did not like the trip as much but he was a good traveler and gave no trouble. He was always happy when he could be with Billy.

Billy had read many cowboy stories and he was excited to see the west. He was even more excited when he saw his first cowboy. The cowboy was riding a big gray horse and he seemed very friendly. He told them that the ranch they were going to was only a few miles farther on. Billy liked the cowboy at once and hoped he would see him again.

When they got to the ranch Billy led Blaze to a big corral. Blaze was so happy when he found that he was going to have such a nice big pasture to play in. It had been a long ride in the little trailer and it felt good to stretch his legs. He knew he was going to like the west.

Bright and early the next day Billy put the western saddle and bridle his father had bought for him on Blaze. He wore his big cowboy hat and his new cowboy boots. He felt like a real cowboy as he started out for a long ride with Blaze. There would be so much to see in this wide open country. Blaze seemed to want to explore, too, for he galloped along gaily toward the blue hills far away.

After riding several miles he came to a big herd of cattle. There was a cowboy nearby. It was the cowboy they had met yesterday. He was very nice and friendly and he told Billy many interesting things about the west. His name was Jim. Billy was anxious to explore the hills so Jim rode along with him.

They had almost reached the hills when they heard shouts and horses galloping. A beautiful black horse was running like the wind with three cowboys chasing after him.

"That's Thunderbolt!" cried Jim. "He's a wild horse everybody is trying to catch but he's too fast for them. Look at him run! Isn't he a beauty?"

Billy was glad to see that the cowboys were falling farther and farther behind. He did not want them to catch that beautiful horse. Jim told him that Thunderbolt was the last of the wild horses. Billy would have liked to follow him up into the hills but he was afraid his mother would worry if he was late for lunch.

Early the next morning Billy started for the hills. Jim had invited Billy to have lunch with him so he could spend the whole day exploring. He had told his father and mother all about Thunderbolt. He hoped to see the wild horse again.

"We're going to look for Thunderbolt," he said to Blaze. "I'd like to see him close, wouldn't you?" Blaze seemed to understand for he galloped faster.

After riding for many miles Billy and Blaze came to the foot of the hills where Jim and the cattle were. While they were eating Billy told Jim that he would like to ride up into the hills and see if he could find Thunderbolt. Jim pointed out a place in the hills where he might see him if he went very quietly.

"I saw him there twice," Jim said.

Billy and Blaze had climbed many of the smaller hills and were coming through some bushes when Blaze stopped suddenly. There, just ahead on a flat ledge, was Thunderbolt! He looked so wild and proud that Billy was sure he had never seen anything so beautiful. Thunderbolt did not see them until Blaze whinnied. Then he turned and snorted. He looked at Billy and Blaze for a moment before he turned and galloped away. He did not seem to be frightened. He seemed to know that this boy and his pony did not mean to harm him.

After that Billy rode over to the hills almost every day. Sometimes he ate with Jim but often he brought his own lunch and ate in the shade of some bush while Blaze ate grass. He would take off the saddle and bridle and let Blaze go where he liked. He knew the pony would always come when he was called. Each day he left some carrots and sugar on the flat rock where he had seen Thunderbolt. They were always gone next day so he felt sure Thunderbolt had been there.

One day he fell asleep after his lunch. He woke up suddenly and there on the flat rock were Blaze and Thunderbolt, side by side, eating the carrots and sugar. When they had finished everything they walked off together.

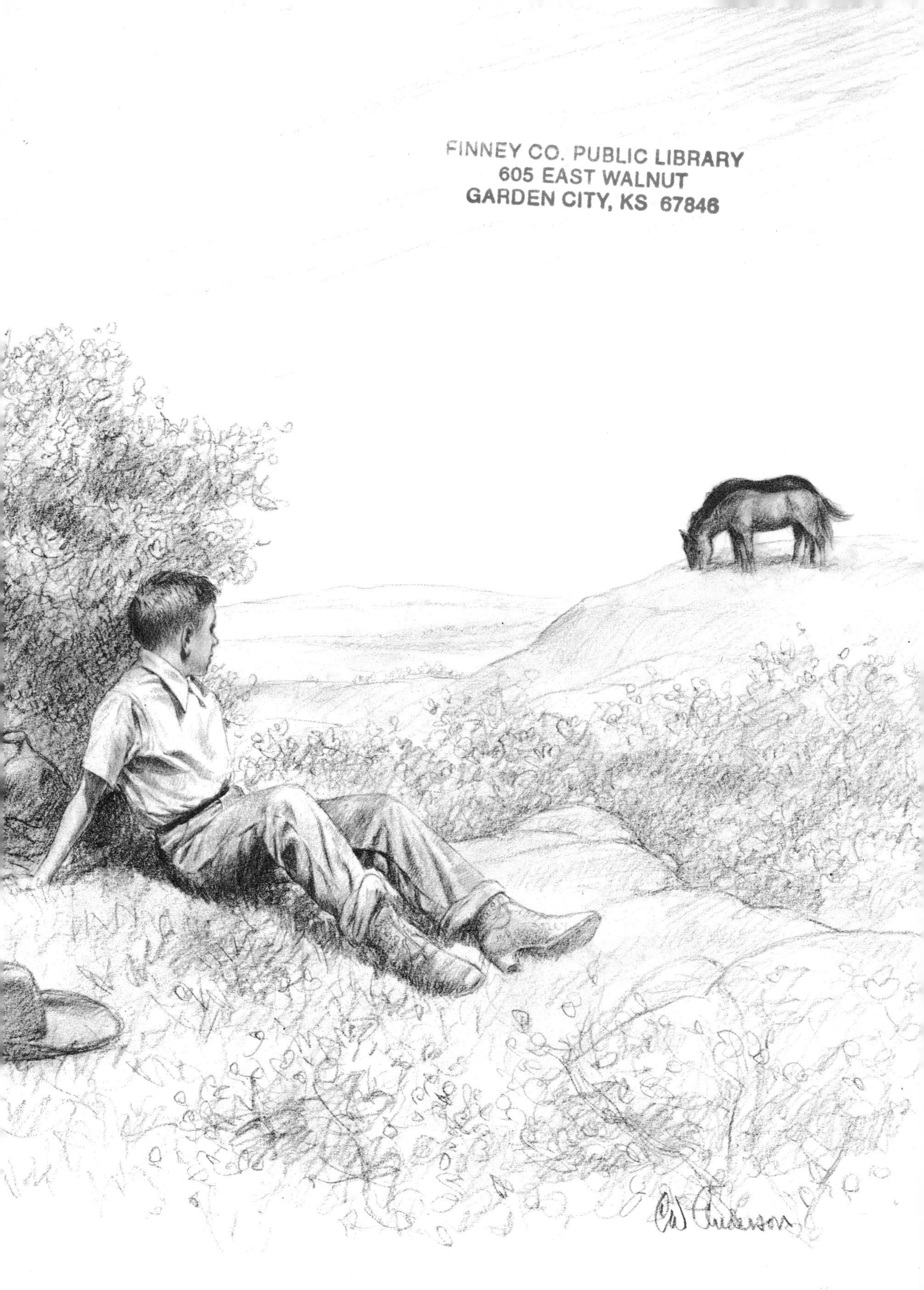
CW Anderson

When Billy called Blaze a little later, he came at once but there was no sign of Thunderbolt. Billy met Jim on his way home and told him what had happened. Jim was very surprised.

"Thunderbolt must be lonesome," he said. "He never sees another horse except those that chase him. Your pony is friendly and he likes him. Be very quiet and don't try to go near him and he may get to know you, too."

Billy dreamed about Thunderbolt that night and for many nights afterwards. Once he even dreamed he was riding the beautiful black horse. The next day he started out earlier than ever for he felt something exciting was going to happen. The nearer they came to the hills the faster Blaze went. Billy knew that Blaze was eager to see his new friend again. When they reached the rock there stood Thunderbolt. This time he didn't run away but stood still and whinnied to Blaze. Billy unsaddled Blaze as quickly as he could and turned him loose. He trotted over to Thunderbolt and Billy could see how glad they were to see each other.

After a while Billy called Blaze so they could start for home. Thunderbolt watched while he was saddling Blaze and then began to follow them. Billy was very excited for he thought Thunderbolt might follow them all the way home. Then maybe he would like the good food he would get and Blaze's company so much that he would stay. But just then Thunderbolt saw some cowboys in the distance and he turned and galloped back into the hills. Billy and Blaze were disappointed. Blaze walked slower than usual for he did not like to leave his friend.

When Billy came to the corral to feed Blaze early the next morning, he thought he must be dreaming. There was Thunderbolt with Blaze. He had come down during the night and jumped into the corral to be with his friend. Billy was very excited and happy.

"If I can only make him want to stay, he will be mine," he said to himself as he hurried to get another bucket with oats for Thunderbolt.

Billy quietly put the two pails of feed in the corral. Soon Blaze and Thunderbolt were having breakfast together. At first Thunderbolt was nervous but when he tasted the oats he forgot all about being frightened. He had never tasted anything so good before. Billy's father and mother were almost as excited as he was. They thought Thunderbolt was the most beautiful horse they had ever seen. His father told Billy to be very quiet and gentle around Thunderbolt and the horse would soon get to know him and trust him.

Billy followed his father's advice and it was not long before he could feed Thunderbolt carrots and sugar from his hand and pat him. When Thunderbolt found that no one was going to harm him or bother him he became very friendly and seemed very happy in his new home. Soon he began to look for Billy as much as Blaze did and to whinny when he saw him.

Often Billy would climb on Blaze's back and ride around the corral. Thunderbolt always followed along beside them. Billy hoped that some day he could ride the beautiful black horse and he wanted him to understand that it would not hurt him if he got on his back. Billy felt sure that no one could ever ride Thunderbolt unless the horse wanted him to.

One day Jim came over and when he saw how quiet Thunderbolt was he said he would try to ride him for Billy. But when Thunderbolt saw Jim coming towards him with his lasso he began to rear and buck.

"He thinks you are one of the cowboys that chased him," cried Billy. "Let me try him. He knows me now and isn't afraid of me."

Billy called Blaze to come over and stand beside Thunderbolt and then he patted the black horse and talked softly to him until he was quiet. Then he quietly climbed on his back. Thunderbolt trembled a little and snorted but he did not buck or kick. He knew Billy and Blaze were his friends. Soon they were walking quietly around the corral. Jim was very surprised and pleased and told Billy that he was going to be a fine horseman.

Billy rode Thunderbolt around the corral for many days before he put a saddle and bridle on him. By that time he trusted Billy, and with Blaze beside him he felt that everything was all right. Soon he knew what he was supposed to do as well as Blaze, and Billy was very proud of him.

Blaze and Thunderbolt became such good friends that they always had to be together. If Billy went for a ride on Blaze, Thunderbolt always came along, and if he rode Thunderbolt, Blaze always galloped happily beside him. Jim was very proud of the way Billy had trained Thunderbolt and told him that now he had the finest horse and the finest pony in that part of the country. Billy was very proud and happy for he felt sure that it was true.

BY C. W. ANDERSON

Billy and Blaze
Blaze and the Gypsies
Blaze and the Forest Fire
Blaze Finds the Trail
Blaze and Thunderbolt
Blaze and the Mountain Lion
Blaze and the Indian Cave
Blaze and the Lost Quarry
Blaze and the Gray Spotted Pony
Blaze Shows the Way